The Hamster from Room 24 is Missing

by Nidia Scott • illustrated by Susan Spellman

Harcourt

Orlando   Boston   Dallas   Chicago   San Diego

Visit *The Learning Site!*

www.harcourtschool.com

There was always something interesting to do in Mrs. Parker's fifth-grade class. Most of the time the class was very busy. They were growing plants for a science project. They were also writing a play about their town.

Near a big window Herman, the class hamster, played in his cage. He liked to climb up high. He ran on his little wheel. He had lots of toys, and he had lots of good things to eat. Herman was popular with the class. Everyone really liked him.

Herman liked to play out of his cage, too. Sometimes Herman climbed to the top of his cage and looked at its door. Then the class knew that he wanted to be out. They let him play on the table.

It was Monday morning—Alex's turn to feed Herman. Alex knew how to take care of hamsters. He was determined to do a good job. Alex filled a clean food bowl with some green leaves, some raisins, and some pieces of apple. He put some seeds in, too. Then he carried the bowl to the cage.

But Herman's cage was empty. Herman was gone!

Alex was determined to find Herman. He turned to his class. "Herman is gone!" he said in a loud, clear voice. "He's not inside his cage."

Mrs. Parker stopped writing on the board. Janey and Steven stopped putting books on the shelves. Lashaun almost dropped his art project.

"Herman is *gone*," Alex said again, in case they didn't hear him the first time.

"Herman didn't run away," Alex thought. "He likes his home. He likes his wheel. He likes Mrs. Parker and the fifth-grade class. Maybe he's sleeping in his tunnel."

Susan and Kenya stopped measuring water for their math project. Jack and Carlos stopped watering the plants for their science experiment.

"Are you sure?" asked Mrs. Parker.

"He's not inside his cage," Alex repeated. "I looked in his tunnel. He's not there. He's not in his sleeping box. He's not under the paper in his cage. *He's really gone!*"

"It's a mystery!" said Steven.

"Hmmm," said Carlos. "The case of the missing hamster."

"Where did he go?" asked Susan. "He doesn't need more water or food. His cage is clean. He has toys."

Alex looked into Herman's cage one more time. He looked at the hamster's empty wheel. It was quiet. Alex was determined to find Herman.

Does anyone have any ideas?" asked Mrs. Parker.

No one spoke.

"Let's think about what hamsters do," said Mrs. Parker. "Who can tell us one thing?"

"They like to check out new places," said Joe. "They like to run around."

Kim said, "They like to eat lots of green food, like leaves and grass. They like many kinds of nuts. Maybe Herman went out to get some."

"Herman likes lots of different things to do," said Steven. "Maybe Herman got bored with his toys. Maybe he got bored with his wheel. Maybe he went looking for something new to do."

"Like what?" Janey asked.

"Like gymnastics!" Steven said.

"Gymnastics?" Janey repeated, putting her hands on her hips.

"Sure!" Steven said. "He loves running around on his wheel. Maybe he wanted to try some new tricks."

"Let's go to the gym!" said Mrs. Parker. "Maybe he is under a soccer ball. Maybe he's asleep in a gym bag."

Alex pictured a happy Herman jumping on the trampoline, doing cartwheels on the mat, trotting across the balance beam.

The gym was empty. Everyone, even Mrs. Parker, took off their shoes at the door. No one could go into the gym without sport shoes. Everyone walked in their socks.

They checked inside the rolled-up mats. They looked under the trampoline. They checked the balance beam. They looked everywhere.

No Herman.

"Maybe he wanted to see the butterflies!" said Janey.

"What butterflies?" asked Carlos.

"The ones he could see outside from the classroom window," Janey answered.

"That's an idea, Janey," said Mrs. Parker. "The weather is warm and sunny. Let's go to the field next to the cafeteria!"

As they walked, Alex imagined a happy Herman outside, jumping through the field, napping in the tall grass, and checking out the bugs on the ground.

"Bug snacks are very popular with hamsters," Alex said.

"Snacks!" said Kim. "I'm sure of it! Herman wants some different snacks. He wants something different to eat!"

But no one answered Kim. The class did not hear her. They were too busy. Everyone walked carefully through the grass. They checked every flower. They looked under logs. They called Herman's name.

No Herman.

"I know!" Carlos said. "Maybe he is on the baseball field!"

"Baseball?" said Janey. "Hamsters don't play baseball."

"But the field is close to our classroom," Alex said, more determined than ever. "He's smart. Maybe he heard us talking about it. Maybe Herman wanted to run around the bases."

"Let's go to the baseball field!" said Mrs. Parker. The students followed her to the baseball field.

Alex pictured a happy Herman rolling a baseball, dancing on one of the bases, hiding in the catcher's mask.

They looked around the baseball bucket, the bases, and the catcher's mask.

No Herman.

"Wait a minute," said Kenya. "Herman loves his little tunnel. Maybe a baseball mitt looks like a tunnel to hamsters."

"Let's check out the mitts," said Steven. "May we do that, Mrs. Parker?" he asked.

Herman wasn't outside. He wasn't in the field. He wasn't in the mitt, or near the baseballs. Where *did* Herman go?

Everyone was worried. They walked back into the school. They sat at their desks. They were very quiet. They missed Herman.

Suddenly, Alex had an idea. "I think I know where Herman is! When we were outside, Kim said, 'Herman wants some different snacks. He wants something different to eat!' I don't think Herman is outdoors."

Everyone looked at Alex. He suddenly felt very important. "Herman is across the hall in Mr. Hom's first grade class. They are doing a science project about trees and nuts. My little brother is in that class. That's how I know about the nuts."

"Now, that's good thinking, Alex!" said Mrs. Parker. "I will check with Mr. Hom. Maybe we can go while his class is outside."

Just then, Mr. Hom knocked on the door and walked in. He was holding a small box in his hands.

"I think this little fellow belongs to you," said Mr. Hom. "We just found him in our science corner. He was putting nuts in his mouth, shells and all!"

"Thank you, Mr. Hom," said Mrs. Parker. "We're so glad Herman is back. We are glad that he is safe." She took the box and looked in.

There was Herman. He looked very funny. He had too many nuts in his mouth.

"Come and look at Herman," she said to the class.

Everybody laughed. Herman really *did* look funny. "Herman looks funny to us," said Mrs. Parker. "But he is just being a hamster. Hamsters like to store food. That means they save it to eat later. Hamsters use their cheek pouches to carry food to their homes."

Mrs. Parker gave the box to Alex. He put Herman back in his cage. He closed the door and checked it twice.

When he sat down in his seat, the rest of the class stood up. They clapped their hands. "Hooray for Kim. Hooray for Alex!" they all shouted.

"Mystery solved," said Carlos. "Mystery solved," said the class.